Abdo & Daughters presents

The Three Stooges

Phony Express

Written by
Elwood Ullman and Monty Collins

Adapted by
Bob Italia

©1991 Norman Maurer Productions, Inc. Columbia Pictures Industries, Inc. All Rights Reserved.

THE THREE STOOGES is a trademark of Norman Maurer Productions, Inc. Published by Abdo & Daughters, 6535 Cecilia Circle, Edina, Minnesota 55439. No part of this book may be reproduced in any form without written permission from the publisher.

Library bound edition distributed by Rockbottom Books, Pentagon Tower, P.O. Box 36036, Minneapolis, Minnesota 55435.

Printed in the United States.

To Our Readers:

The Three Stooges performed a brand of comedy known as "slapstick." They used harmless props and horseplay. The Stooges practiced their slapstick routines many times before filming. Their silly behavior is intended for laughs.

LIBRARY OF CONGRESS CATALOGING-IN-PUBLICATION DATA

Italia, Robert, 1955-
    Phony Express / created by Elwood Ullman and Monty Collins; written by Elwood Ullman and Monty Collins; adapted by Bob Italia
       p. cm. — (The Three Stooges)
    Adaptation of the motion picture.
    "Library bound edition"--T.p. verso.
    Summary: Back in the Old West, the Three Stooges make an incompetent attempt to foil a gang of bank robbers.
    ISBN 1-56239-162-3
    [1. Robbers and outlaws -- Fiction. 2. West (U.S.) -- Fiction. 3. Humorous stories.] I. Ullman, Elwood. II. Collins, Monty, 1898-1951. III. Phony Express (Motion picture) IV. Title. V. Series; Italia, Robert, 1955- Three Stooges.
PZ7.I897Ph 1992   [Fic]--dc20   92-11181

International Standard Book Number:
1-56239-162-3

Library of Congress Catalog Card Number:
92-11181

Phony Express

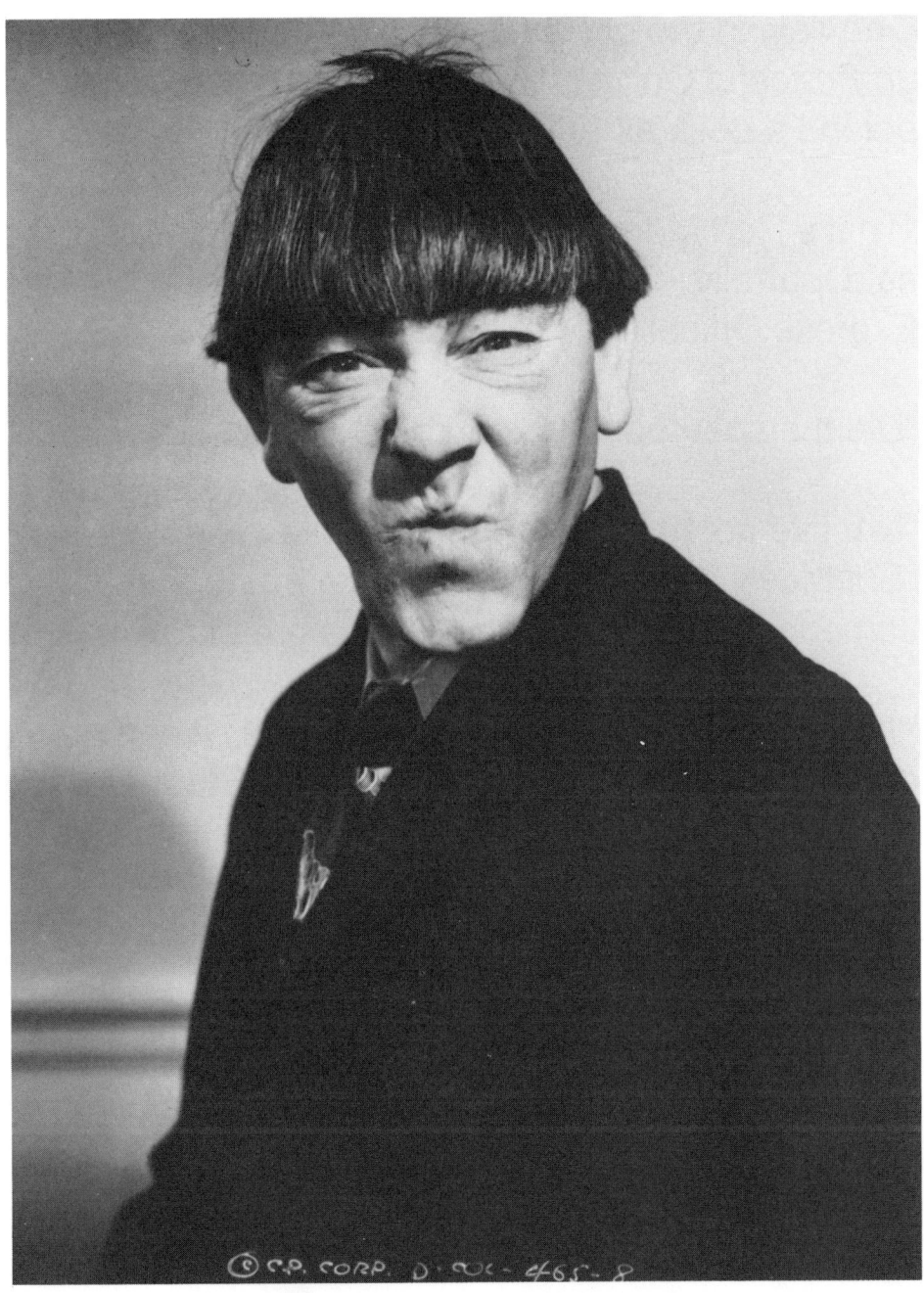

"Oh boy - we're in business!"

The Three Stooges

One day, in the old west, outlaws began shooting up Peaceful Gulch. Two men in an office huddled behind a desk as bullets flew overhead.

"That's Red Morgan and his gang!" Higgins said fearfully. "Last night they robbed the Express Office!"

"Did they get the mine payroll?" Frank said.

"No, I've got that in my bank," replied Higgins. "But they'll be after it next. We've got to find somebody to run these hoodlums out of town."

"There must be someone," Frank said. Then he spotted a wanted poster of the Three Stooges. His eyes brightened. "I've got it! I'll print this picture in the paper and say that they're three famous marshals coming to clean up the town."

"It might work," Higgins said. "It'll give me time to get rid of the payroll."

Meanwhile, in another part of town, the Three Stooges stopped at a salesman's covered wagon.

Phony Express

"Here you are, gentlemen," the salesman said. "Abdul's Cactus Remedy. Cures every ailment known to man or beast. Only one dollar."

"Hey, Moe," Curly said. "Buy me a bottle. I can't sleep."

"What do you mean?" Moe said. "You sleep twelve hours every night."

"Yeah," Curly replied, "but I'm wide awake all day."

"Why you," Moe said angrily. He poked Curly in the eyes.

"Oh!" Curly shouted. Then he barked at Moe.

"Say, I've got to send a telegram," the salesman said. "Will you boys watch my show? Whatever you sell is yours."

Moe rubbed his hands together. "Oh boy," he said, "we're in business!"

As the salesman departed, the Stooges climbed aboard the back of the wagon. Larry and Curly knocked over the remedy bottles.

The Three Stooges

"You lunk heads," Moe snapped. "You broke all the bottles. Get in there and make some more remedy while I do some selling."

Larry and Curly went inside the covered wagon. Moe turned to the gathering crowd.

"All right, here you are, folks," Moe said. "Abdul's Cactus Remedy...good for hay fever, spotted fever and buck fever—and what a bargain for a buck! A cure for colic and rickets. Brightens the teeth. Shines your old silverware. And a definite cure for dandruff and lumbago."

Phony Express

"I'll take a bottle," said a man with a mustache.

Moe frowned. "Go away son, you bother me." Then Moe realized the man was the sheriff. "Sorry, friend, I don't think it would do you any good."

The sheriff grew angry. "You said it would cure lumbago—and I got it!"

"Well, if you're going to stand on a technicality," Moe said nervously. "I'll see my colleague-ees in the clinic."

Meanwhile, inside the wagon, Larry and Curly looked around in confusion.

"Do you know anything about mixing medicines, Doctor?" Larry said to Curly.

"Why, *soi*-tan-ly, Professor," Curly said. "All you got to do is mix a little of this and a little of that."

Larry picked up a jug. "Say, we got plenty of this."

"Then I'll try that," Curly said. He took the jug and poured its contents into a tall glass.

"How about this?" Larry said, handing Curly a bottle.

"Yes, I'll try that." Curly poured more liquid into the glass. The liquid changed into different colors.

"Here's another," Larry said, handing Curly a bottle of pills.

Curly dumped the pills into the glass. The liquid bubbled and smoked. Curly waved his hand at the glass, then barked.

"Oh, boy," Larry exclaimed, "that's hot stuff!"

"That's what he needs for his lumbago," Curly said.

Larry handed Curly an empty bottle. "Here, bottle it."

Curly filled the bottle, then shoved it through an opening in the cover. Meanwhile, Moe continued his salespitch.

"Hey," The sheriff shouted, "how about my bottle? If it don't cure me..." The sheriff ran his finger across his neck.

Moe gulped. "I was afraid of that," he said.

Moe turned toward the covered part of the wagon and grabbed the bottle from Curly. "Here you are, Sheriff," Moe said, handing the bottle to the sheriff. "That'll pick you right up."

"And lay you right down, too," Curly said, poking his head out.

The sheriff took a drink from the bottle. Suddenly, his eyes widened. His mustache spun 'round and 'round and he fell to the ground. When the sheriff sat up, smoke trailed from his mouth. "I've been poisoned!" he shouted.

Moe rushed to the front of the wagon. "Step on the gas," he said to Larry and Curly.

Curly grabbed the reins. "Giddeap!" he shouted at the horses. The wagon rumbled down the street.

The Three Stooges

"Hey, you—come back!" the sheriff cried. The sheriff threw the remedy bottle at the wagon.

Suddenly, the wagon blew up, leaving the Stooges in tattered clothes.

Phony Express

"We're here to clean up the joint."

The next day, three outlaws stood outside a saloon reading a newspaper. Suddenly they saw a photograph of the Three Stooges. The headline read:

WILD BILL HICCUP DUE IN.

"Wait'll Red hears about this," an outlaw said fearfully. "I wonder when the marshals get here?"

Then the Three Stooges appeared. "Say, pardner," Curly said, slapping an outlaw on the shoulder, "will you tell me where I can find—"

The outlaws looked at the Stooges, then ran into the saloon.

Moe glared at Curly. "Why don't you change that face of yours? You scare people."

Curly waved at Moe.

Just then, Moe saw a poster outside the saloon that read: **PORTER WANTED.** "Hey, looks like you guys are going to work. Make yourselves presentable."

Phony Express

The Stooges brushed the dust off each other. Then Larry and Curly went through the swinging doors of the saloon. Moe followed them. The swinging doors hit him in the face.

"Hey, Red," an outlaw shouted, handing Red the newspaper, "get a load of this!"

Red grabbed the newspaper and looked at the photograph of the Three Stooges. "Wild Bill Hiccup," he said nervously.

"We'd better call off stickin' up that bank," an outlaw said.

"We'll knock that bank over before the marshals get here," Red replied.

"Look," an outlaw shouted, "they're here already."

The Stooges approached. "Who's boss around here?" Moe said.

"Why?" Red asked fearfully.

"We're here to clean up the joint."

13

The Three Stooges

"Now, now, take it easy, boys," Red said nervously. "H-Have a drink on me."

"*Soi*-tan-ly!" Curly said. The Stooges rushed the bar.

Suddenly, an attractive young woman approached Curly. "Hello, tall, dark and handsome," she said. "Shall we trip the light fantastic?"

Phony Express

"I'd rather dance," Curly said, taking along his drink.

Curly and the woman danced in the center of the saloon. When Curly tried to twirl the woman around, he spilled his drink down her back. The woman screamed and pulled away, trying to shake the drink from her dress.

Curly thought the woman was still dancing. "Oh, fancy hey?" he said. "Get a load of this." Trying to impress the woman, Curly shuffled backward until his spur poked Red in the rump. Red screamed as he jumped from his chair.

Suddenly, a waiter approached Red. "Red, get a load of that." He showed Red the Stooges' old wanted poster. "I thought these guys were phonies!"

Red grew angry. "I'll stop his hiccup." He drew his gun and held it under Curly's nose. Then Red shot the glass from Larry's hand. "Now let's see how good a shot *you* are," Red said to Curly.

Curly drew a slingshot from his holster. He aimed at a row of bottles on the bar.

"Not with that," Moe said angrily, knocking the slingshot from Curly's hand, "with a gun!" He took Red's gun and handed it to Curly.

Meanwhile, Larry ducked behind the bar with a hammer in hand. Curly closed his eyes and fired. Larry reached up and broke a bottle with the hammer.

"Did I do that?" Curly said.

"Certainly," Moe replied. "Now take the next three in rapid fire."

Curly fired three times. Larry reached up with the hammer and broke three bottles. Red couldn't believe what he was seeing.

Curly laughed. "I'll take the next one the hard way." He pulled the trigger, but the gun didn't fire. Larry reached up and broke another bottle. Red glared at Moe and Curly.

"Huh," Moe said nervously. "He scared it to death."

Red drew his gun on the Stooges. Frightened, Curly fired a shot in the air. The bullet struck a ceiling lamp which fell on Red's head. As Red slumped in a chair, the Stooges ran from the saloon. They were safe—for now.

The Three Stooges

"Nyuk-nyuk-nyuk!"

Phony Express

That evening, Higgins hired the Stooges to guard his bank. "Now remember, men," he said, handing them some rifles, "you've been deputized to guard my bank. Protect it with your lives—or else!" Higgins trudged off.

The Stooges tried to enter the bank, but Red—already inside the bank—blocked the door. "You can't come in here," he said.

"Why not?" Curly asked.

"Can't you read?" Red said, pointing to the sign on the door. "Open ten to three."

"Oh, we're sorry," Moe said. "We'll be back in the morning." The Stooges turned away as Red closed the door.

Moe stood between Larry and Curly as they marched down the street. "Hip, hup—left face!" Moe cried.

Larry turned left, but Curly turned right—hitting Moe in the head with the rifle.

"You cabbage head," Moe shouted at Curly, "I said left face!"

The Three Stooges

"Oh!" Curly said. He turned left and again hit Moe in the head.

"Wait a minute, you!" Moe said angrily. "What did I say before?"

"Left face," Curly replied.

"All right," Moe said. "This time make it right face."

Curly spun to the right and hit Moe in the head with the rifle. "Come here!" Moe shouted, grabbing the rifle from Curly. "Now, right face!"

Phony Express

Curly spun away from Moe. Moe raised the rifle and hit Curly over the head. "How did that feel?" Moe said.

"How did *what* feel?" Curly replied, turning to Moe.

Moe slapped Curly in the face. "That," he said.

Suddenly, the Stooges heard an explosion. "What was that?" Larry said.

"The bank!" Moe shouted. "Come on!"

The Stooges rushed to the bank. There was a gaping hole in the front wall.

"*Oh*-hhh," Curly said, looking at the hole. "Hey look—termites! And big ones, too!"

"Come on," Moe said, "we got to get in."

The Stooges tried to enter the front door, but it was locked. Meanwhile, Red and his gang sneaked out the bank through the gaping hole.

"We'll have to use force, men," Moe said. "Heave, holt!" The Stooges broke the door down and entered the bank.

The Three Stooges

Just then, Higgins appeared outside the bank. "Help, help," he shouted. "Robbers!" Higgins entered the bank.

A crowd gathered outside. Suddenly, the Stooges emerged with a man they were holding. The man's jacket covered his face.

"There you are, folks," Moe said proudly to the crowd. "We've got the robber!"

The man pulled the jacket from his face. It was Higgins. "So, you've got the robber, eh?" Higgins said in anger.

If the Stooges wanted to stay out of jail, they would have to find Red and his gang.

Phony Express

"If we don't get that payroll back by tonight, they're gonna lynch us!"

The Three Stooges

The Stooges were in the woods outside Peaceful Gulch, looking for Red and his gang. Curly was on his hands and knees, sniffing the ground and howling like a bloodhound. Larry held the leash as he and Moe followed Curly.

"Mush, mush!" Moe shouted at Curly. "You know, if we don't get that payroll back by tonight, they're gonna lynch us."

"Get 'em, boy," Larry said. "Pick up the trail!"

Suddenly, Curly stopped. He sniffed the ground harder, then let out a growl.

"He's on the trail of those skunks!" Moe cried. "He's got the scent!"

Curly led them to a tiny cave. "It must be their hideout," Moe said. "Get 'em!"

Curly growled and barked as he stuck his head into the tiny opening. Then he began digging wildly, throwing dirt into Moe's face.

Finally, when the opening was big enough, Curly crawled into the cave. Moe and Larry heard growling and snarling. Suddenly, all was quiet.

Phony Express

Moe pulled the leash, but it had been cut. "By golly," Moe said, "they got him."

Just then, Curly crawled from the cave. "Nyuk-nyuk-nyuk," he said, wearing a skunk-skin cap.

"Get up—*get up!*" Moe shouted. "Why you skunk!"

"Hey, fellas," Larry said, "look—a cabin!"

"Let's go!" Moe said. The Stooges rushed to the log cabin and entered the front door. In the center of the room was a potbelly stove. Steel traps hung from the walls.

"There's nobody home," Larry said.

"Let's look around," Moe shouted. "Search the joint. Spread out!"

Curly opened a clothes chest and found a box of mothballs. He picked up the box and opened it. "*Oh*-hhh!" he said. 'Pepperminties!"

Curly popped a mothball into his mouth and chewed. "*Hm*-mmm!" he said with delight. Then he put a handful of mothballs into his mouth.

Curly approached Moe who was on his hands and knees looking under a bed. Curly stepped on a loose floorboard. The board sprung up and smacked Moe in the jaw.

"Hey fellas," Larry cried, pointing to the hole in the floor, "look—the payroll money!"

Phony Express

Moe reached in the hole. "Oh boy," he said, pulling out bags of money, "oh my, oh my. There's gold in them thar hills."

"Nyuk-nyuk-nyuk," said Curly. "There's gold in them thar floors, too."

Just then, the Stooges heard Red and his men approaching the cabin.

"It's the guys!" Moe shouted. "They're coming back! Quick—hide the dough!"

The Stooges dumped the money bags into the potbelly stove.

The Three Stooges

"Hurry up, let's go!" Moe hollered.

Standing at the potbelly stove, Curly watched Moe and Larry leave the cabin. "Nyuk-nyuk-nyuk," he said with a smile as he dipped his hand into the stove.

Moe sneaked up behind Curly and pulled him away from the stove. Curly backed into a steel trap on the wall. The trap snapped shut on his pants. "Hey Moe," Curly cried, "they got me!"

Moe growled as he approached Curly. "Turn around here," he said. "Easy now, I'll have you out in a second." Moe tore the trap from Curly's pants. Then Moe's eyes brightened with an idea. "I've got it—the traps!"

"You mean I got it, the traps," Curly said, rubbing his behind in pain.

Moe grabbed some steel traps from the wall. "Get the rest of them," he said to Larry and Curly. Then they rushed out the front door.

"You guys lay those traps down the path," Moe said as he set some traps on the ground. "Hurry up!"

Phony Express

The Stooges buried the traps under some leaves. Then they stood in the path. Red and his gang approached the cabin, and entered the back door.

"Hey," Red shouted, looking at the empty hole in the floor, "we've been robbed! Find the crooks!" Red and another man ran out the back door.

The rest of the gang rushed out the front door. They saw the Stooges standing on the path.

"Hey!" Curly said, waving his hand at the outlaws. "Nyuk-nyuk-nyuk."

Angered, the outlaws charged the Stooges. But as they did, they stepped on the steel traps. "Help, help, help!" the outlaws cried as they tried to remove the traps. But they were caught.

"Hurry up, kid!" Moe said to Curly. "Go back and get the dough!"

Curly ran into the cabin and locked the back door. Then he reached into the potbelly stove. Suddenly, he heard someone banging on the back door.

The Three Stooges

"Hey, open up!" the man's voice said. "It's Red!"

Curly got nervous and looked for a place to hide.

"Hey, somebody must be in there," Red shouted. "Come on, let's break the door down!"

Curly climbed into the potbelly stove just as Red and his friend broke the door down.

"Somebody got the dough," Red's friend said.

"Yeah," Red said, puffing on his cigar, "we've been double-crossed. Take a look around."

Red removed the cigar from his mouth. He opened the lid on the potbelly stove and dropped the cigar inside. The cigar landed on a piece of paper behind Curly. The paper ignited, and the flame touched Curly's gunbelt.

Suddenly, the bullets on the gunbelt went off. The potbelly stove spun wildly as bullets and sparks showered the cabin. Red and his friend hit the floor, then rushed from the cabin.

Phony Express

When all the bullets had gone off, Curly climbed out of the stove with the money. The Stooges had recaptured the stolen payroll!

The Three Stooges

"I'm tryin' to think but nothin' happens!"